But I Love my Clothes

T0309438

Written by Juliet Clare Bell

Illustrated by Jordan Kincaid

Collins

Who and what is in this story?

clothes

T-shirt

Jake

Listen and say

hat

Sam

jeans

It's morning. Sam is choosing her clothes.

Sam says, "I love my blue T-shirt and my blue jeans and my blue hat!"

This is Sam's brother, Jake.

Jake says, "Oh dear, Sam. You are big, but your clothes are very small!"

They look at Sam's clothes again.
Sam says, "Oh no! My clothes *ARE*
too small."

Jake says, "You need new clothes."
Sam says, "I don't want new clothes.
I love my clothes!"

There are lots of clothes at the shop.
And lots of colours.

Sam chooses some clothes.

Jake says, "You're big, but you're not *that* big!"

Sam tries again.

Sam says, "That's good!"

Jake says, "Try a *new* colour, Sam".

Jake says, "Why don't you try red ... or green ... or yellow?"

Sam says, "I don't like *these* colours, but ..."

"... I *would* like a new colour. Don't look!"

Sam says, "You're right, Jake.
I LOVE *this* new colour!"

Jake says, "But they're blue too!"

Sam says, "Yes, but they're a *new* colour blue. See? I love my new clothes! Thank you, Jake."

Picture dictionary

Listen and repeat

clothes

hat

jeans

T-shirt

small

big

1 Look and order the story

2 Listen and say

Collins

Published by Collins
An imprint of HarperCollins*Publishers*
Westerhill Road
Bishopbriggs
Glasgow
G64 2QT

HarperCollins*Publishers*
1st Floor, Watermarque Building
Ringsend Road
Dublin 4
Ireland

William Collins' dream of knowledge for all began with the publication of his first book in 1819.

A self-educated mill worker, he not only enriched millions of lives, but also founded a flourishing publishing house. Today, staying true to this spirit, Collins books are packed with inspiration, innovation and practical expertise. They place you at the centre of a world of possibility and give you exactly what you need to explore it.

© HarperCollins*Publishers* Limited 2020

10 9 8 7 6 5 4 3 2

ISBN 978-0-00-839758-6

Collins® and COBUILD® are registered trademarks of HarperCollins*Publishers* Limited

www.collins.co.uk/elt

British Library Cataloguing in Publication Data

A catalogue record for this publication is available from the British Library.

Author: Juliet Clare Bell
Illustrator: Jordan Kincaid (Beehive)
Series editor: Rebecca Adlard
Publishing manager: Lisa Todd
Product managers: Jennifer Hall and Caroline Green
In-house editor: Alma Puts Keren
Project manager: Emily Hooton
Editor: Frances Amrani
Proofreaders: Natalie Murray and Michael Lamb
Cover designer: Kevin Robbins
Typesetter: 2Hoots Publishing Services Ltd
Audio produced by id audio, London
Reading guide author: Emma Wilkinson
Production controller: Rachel Weaver
Printed and bound by: GPS Group, Slovenia

Download the audio for this book and a reading guide for parents and teachers at www.collins.co.uk/839758